The Ghost of Nicholas Greebe

Tony Johnston

pictures by S. D. Schindler

PUFFIN BOOKS

For Jeanne and Wray Cornwell, who shared their ghost with me,
and in memory of Margot Tomes
—T. J.

To Amelia Lau Carling and Michele Foley
—S. D. S.

 # EFic 3·27·02

PUFFIN BOOKS
Published by the Penguin Group
Penguin Putnam Books for Young Readers, 345 Hudson Street, New York, NY 10014, U.S.A.
Penguin Books Ltd, 27 Wrights Lane, London W8 5TZ, England
Penguin Books Australia Ltd, Ringwood, Victoria, Australia
Penguin Books Canada Ltd, 10 Alcorn Avenue, Toronto, Ontario, Canada M4V 3B2
Penguin Books (N.Z.) Ltd, 182-190 Wairau Road, Auckland 10, New Zealand

Penguin Books Ltd, Registered Offices: Harmondsworth, Middlesex, England

First published in the United States of America
by Dial Books for Young Readers, a division of Penguin Books USA Inc., 1996
Published by Puffin Books, a member of Penguin Putnam Books for Young Readers, 1999

1 3 5 7 9 10 8 6 4 2

Text copyright © Tony Johnston, 1996 Illustrations copyright © S. D. Schindler, 1996
All rights reserved

THE LIBRARY OF CONGRESS HAS CATALOGED THE DIAL EDITION AS FOLLOWS:
Johnston, Tony, date / The ghost of Nicholas Greebe /
by Tony Johnston; pictures by S. D. Schindler.—1st ed. p. cm.
Summary: In Colonial Massachusetts, the ghost of a recently buried farmer haunts
his widow's house after a dog takes one of his bones on a long journey.
ISBN 0-8037-1648-6(hc. trade) ISBN 0-8037-1649-4(lib.)
[1. Ghosts—Fiction. 2. Bones—Fiction. 3. Dogs—Fiction.] I. Schindler, S. D., date, ill. II. Title.
PZ7.J6478Gh 1996 [Fic]—dc20 95-35324 CIP AC

Puffin Books ISBN 0-14-056267-2

Printed in the United States of America

The artwork for each painting was prepared with ink.

In Colonial times, quiet Massachusetts valleys—dark with trees, threaded with rivers, and often cloaked in fog—gave rise to thoughts of the supernatural. There, among hidden hills, tales of haunts and ghosts abounded. Tales such as this one. . . .

Toward year's end, above a rambling farmhouse, the moon rose cold and still. It shone through a window and onto the bed within, where the farmer Nicholas Greebe lay sleeping. In the luminous gloom, precisely at midnight, the old man gave up the ghost. That is to say, he died.

The next day dawned exceedingly cold. Unfortunately (as we shall later see) his shivering family hurriedly dug a grave, buried him with a prayer, and hastened back to the warmth of the fire.

Outside, beneath pewter skies, Nicholas Greebe was left to rest. A headstone with an angel marked his grave.

One year later to the very day, the family gathered at the farm. Everyone feasted and toasted the departed man. In the midst of the festivities—and by peculiar coincidence at the very stroke of twelve—a little dog felt the desire to go outside.

As if by some mysterious plan, the animal trotted straight to Nicholas Greebe's shallow grave. He dug feverishly, heaping a pile of moon-silvered earth behind him. Suddenly he found something thin and hard with knobby knobs on the ends—the bone of Nicholas Greebe.

Just as the dog started back with his prize, a carriage stopped in the middle
of the road. While the passengers alighted to gaze at the moon, the curious
little dog scampered up to the carriage, climbed the steps, and slipped beneath
a seat. Worn out from digging, he fell asleep.

Presently the people returned and the carriage rumbled off, with passengers, dog, and bone. As they melted into the night, something luminous and white arose from the grave of Nicholas Greebe. It floated into the farmhouse, settled itself in a chair before the fire, and lifted its voice in a resonant moan:

From this night forth
I quest, I quest,
till all my bones
together rest.

At once everyone stopped toasting and began shrieking. They rushed to their carriages and rattled away, scattering down the dark country lanes like leaves before wild wind.

Only Nicholas Greebe's frightened widow remained—and his unhappy ghost.

The ghost began to haunt the farm, looking for the lost bone. Its restless rambles took it from one corner of the place to another. Sometimes something unseen set hens fluttering upon their nests. Sometimes something caused the lids of the kitchen stove to rise as if by levitation. Sometimes an unearthly wind whined in the corn. And ceaseless wailing filled the night:

Forevermore
I quest, I quest,
till all my bones
together rest.

While Nicholas Greebe's ghost searched in vain, the pilfered bone had begun a remarkable journey. The mysterious carriage made for Boston, clattering straight to the wharf. There, one of its passengers, a sea captain, boarded a whaler bound for the Polar North—and right behind him went the little dog, holding fast to the bone all the while. Once aboard, he sniffed a few sniffs, found a good spot, and quickly hid his treasure.

Just as the whaler was departing, the dog, sparked by the excitement, began dashing about the decks, barking. "Great smacking flukes!" cried a sailor. "What's this?" And he set the dog ashore.

So the ship sailed, but the dog remained, grieving for the bone. Grieving like the ghost of Nicholas Greebe.

Month after cold month passed. The whaler cut through the perilous waters of the Horn and sailed north, ever north, toward Alaska. Strangely, on the entire voyage not a trace of a single whale was seen, neither barnacle nor blow.

Bored as blubber, one sailor searched for something to carve to pass the time. By oddest chance (or was it?) he came upon an object tucked into a shadowy corner—something thin and hard, with knobby knobs on the ends. The bone of Nicholas Greebe!

The sailor decorated the bone with a scrimshaw ship, a present for his sweetheart when once again they met.

But that was not to be. For soon after, on a night ghostly with fog,
the whaler struck an iceberg and sank like a stone.

The very next day there came a fisherman, gliding silently on a large ice floe. By a fantastic fluke, he stopped just where the ship had gone down and flung out his net. Along with a mess of shiny fish, what else should he retrieve? Marvel of marvels—the bone of Nicholas Greebe!

Sorely in need of supplies, he rushed to a trading post and exchanged the bone for goods. So the bone came to rest—for the moment—between bladder floats and stacks of pelts.

Now all the time that the bone was traveling, the ghost still haunted the farm, day and night, night and day. And every year on the eve of the theft, it settled itself before the fire once again:

Forevermore
I quest, I quest,
till all my bones
together rest.

One hundred years passed in this way. *Precisely one hundred years.* On a night like that other night so long ago, a great moon rose. Its pale light washed the trees a spectral white.

Inside the farmhouse a family was gathered. The son had returned to be married, a sailor home from the sea. From far-off Alaska he had brought a satchel full of gifts, which he set down by the hearth.

Just as the wedding began, a little dog snoozing by the fire awoke. He sniffed a few sniffs, made straight for the satchel, and began chewing happily. Soon he had chewed the handle off.

He trotted it outside, dug a hole, and quickly buried his prize—a thin, hard
object adorned with a spidery scrimshaw ship and knobby knobs on the ends.
Bought at a trading post for use as a handle, it had at last come home—
the bone of Nicholas Greebe!

Suddenly, from nowhere and from everywhere at once, thunder clapped, lightning forked and flared. Every lamp guttered as if blown by bodiless breath. Then, flapping like an empty sleeve, the ghost appeared and declared:

This very hour
I end my quest.
My bones once more
together rest.

So saying, it was gone.

But this was not the end of the tale.

Not long afterward, someone chanced to stroll through the graveyard and noticed something that to this day goes utterly unexplained: The angel on Nicholas Greebe's headstone had vanished. In its place a little dog was carved in the stone. And in his mouth he held—a bone.

In memory of
Nicholas
Greebe

born
1692

died
17